Natalie Jane Prior lives in inner-city Brisbane with her dog Ragnar and husband Peter, with whom she runs a business selling wooden recorders. Her interests include reading, gardening, going to the theater and eating chocolate. A former librarian, she now writes full-time.

Thank you to my mother, who sent me to dance classes

I owe a big 'thank you' to lots of other people too.

At the Queensland Ballet, I talked to Kay Francis, Jane Murphy, Harold Collins, Benita Whalley, Terry Walduck, and dancers Terri-Lee Milne, Graham Fletcher, Julian Lankshear, Michelle Giammichele and Matthew Thomson; thanks also to Angus Lugsdin of the Queensland Dance School of Excellence and his students Trisha Shorten and Michael Kopp. Sue Bursztynski, Greg Rogers and Shirley Baker all made it possible for me to write the section on Renaissance dance; and Angie O'Toole (Rasheeda's Veils), Yani, Emma Baker-Spink, Megan Banach, Laurel Victoria Gray and Sarah Murray-White helped me with the chapter on belly dancing. Other people who helped include Joie Sumby, Tirtharaj Dasa and Nicola Oliver; and Rosalind Price and Sarah Brenan at Allen & Unwin. Finally, Valerie Lisner made valuable suggestions and read parts of the manuscript to check for mistakes. To her and Mary Heath, I owe a debt of thanks for trying to teach me ballet when I was an awkward, unco-ordinated little girl. They may not have succeeded in teaching me to dance, but they did teach me how to love it. I hope this book repays them for their efforts.

DANCE Crazy

Star Turns from
Ballet to Belly Dancing

Natalie Jane Prior

A LITTLE
ARK
BOOK

ALLEN & UNWIN

© text, Natalie Jane Prior, 1995
© b/w illustrations, Beth Norling, 1995

First published in 1995
A Little Ark Book, Allen & Unwin Pty Ltd
Distributed in the U.S.A. by Independent Publishers Group, 814 North Franklin Street, Chicago, IL. 60610, Phone 312 337 0747, Fax 312 337 5985,
Internet: ipgbook@mcs.com
Distributed in Canada by McClelland & Stewart, 481 University Avenue, Suite 900, Toronto, ON M5G 2E9, Phone 416 598 1114, Fax 416 598 4002

10 9 8 7 6 5 4 3 2 1

National Library of Australia
Cataloguing-in-Publication entry:

Prior, Natalie Jane, 1963 - .
    Dance crazy: star turns from ballet to belly dancing.

    Bibliography.
    Includes index.
    ISBN 1 86373 929 7

1. Queensland Ballet - Juvenile literature. 2. Dance - Juvenile literature. 3. Dancers - Biography - Juvenile literature. 4. Ballet - Queensland - Juvenile literature. I. Title. (Series: True stories (St. Leonards, N.S.W.)).

792.8

Designed and typeset by Site-Design/Illustration
Printed by McPherson's Printing Group

Photo credits

Thanks to Catherine O'Rourke for photo research
Cover images of Juliet Annan and David Tyndall, final-year students, School of Dance, Victorian College of the Arts, 1995; photo by Jeff Busby, reproduced with permission
Photos of Terri-Lee Milne with Graham Fletcher and of Queensland Ballet wardrobe department by Phillippe Hargreaves, reproduced by permission of the Queensland Ballet
Photo of Rippon Lea Renaissance Dancers by Kathleen Lanigan   Photo of Yani by Jo Hoy   Photo of Ripponlea primary school dance by Ron Ryan (Coo-ee Picture Library)
Photo of Anna Pavlova from Coo-ee Historical Picture Library

Contents

A DANCING WORLD

Introduction

 Everybody is born with a talent. For some people it is the ability to run or swim quickly, for others, the ability to work with their hands, draw beautiful pictures or write stories.

Most people know what their talents are, and go out of their way to use them — after all, everyone enjoys doing what they're good at. But few people have to start building on their natural ability at such an early age as dancers.

Dancers usually begin their training at around six or eight years old (a little later for boys). Typically they will begin with lessons in a local dance academy. Pupils who are there simply for fun or exercise will drop out and move on to other things, but a handful who have both talent *and* determination will carry their training on and eventually take up the grueling life of a professional dancer.

A dancer's life is a hard one. Long days in the studio are followed by performances at night, and often, exhausting tours that leave the dancer physically and mentally worn out. Few dancers can expect their career to last more than 20 years. Like sports stars, dancers put enormous strain on their bodies and are at constant risk of terrible injury; but unlike sports stars, few dancers are well paid for their risks. Yet most dancers believe the hard work, discipline and sacrifice they put into their careers is worth it.

This is not a book about how to dance. If you want to learn basic steps, technique and routines, you should enrol with a good teacher for some lessons. What you will find in this book are true stories about many types of dancers and dancing. Some of the stories are exciting, some of them sad or funny. All of them are about the ambition and commitment of some amazing human beings — and the joy that dancing gives them.

A Working Ballet Company

In Rehearsal

●●●●●●

It's nine o'clock, and the working day has just begun. In the shops and offices across the road from the Thomas Dixon Centre — home of the Queensland Ballet in Australia — people are turning on their word processors, opening their mail and counting the money in their tills. For the dancers of the Queensland Ballet, however, the day's work begins in quite a different way.

Every morning at this time the studio fills with dancers in leotards and old practice clothes, beginning warm-up exercises to prepare for their daily class. Like athletes, dancers have to stay in peak physical condition, and all dancers, even the most famous ones, start their day with

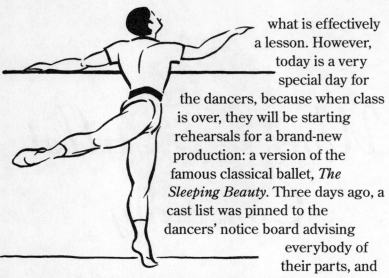

what is effectively a lesson. However, today is a very special day for the dancers, because when class is over, they will be starting rehearsals for a brand-new production: a version of the famous classical ballet, *The Sleeping Beauty*. Three days ago, a cast list was pinned to the dancers' notice board advising everybody of their parts, and now everyone is looking forward to learning new roles.

Among the dancers assembled in the studio this morning are the people who will be dancing the important principal roles. Graham Fletcher has been dancing male principal roles for two years now. He will be dancing the role of the Prince, who awakens Princess Aurora from her hundred-year sleep. His Sleeping Beauty is Terri-Lee Milne. From a distance, Terri-Lee looks small and delicate like the princess whose part she will be dancing, but like all dancers, she is actually very muscular and fit. She too has danced principal roles before. She has known she will be dancing Princess Aurora since she was called in to pose for a publicity photo just over a week ago. Beside her is another dancer, an exotic-looking blonde with huge pale blue eyes. Michelle Giammichele is a very experienced dancer who has worked overseas as well as in Australia. She will be taking the difficult and important role of

Aurora's enemy, the wicked fairy Carabosse who places the baby princess under a curse. On alternate nights she will be dancing the part of Princess Aurora herself.

These people have been chosen by the company's artistic director as the first cast: the dancers who will perform the leading roles on opening night. But in fact there is not one Sleeping Beauty — there are three! Dancing such a huge role night after night would be too much for one dancer, so three casts are taught the main roles, and all the dancers are expected to learn several parts. (This means that if a dancer is injured, or becomes ill, there is always another person who can dance the role.) In big dance companies, a principal dancer will be given a night off to rest after dancing a leading role; but the Queensland Ballet employs only 18 full-time dancers, so everyone has to perform every night. Last night's Prince might be this evening's chief rat!

> *There is not one Sleeping Beauty – there are three!*

One member of the company who is looking forward to this challenge very much is Matthew Thomson. This is Matthew's first year as a professional dancer, although he was lucky enough to perform with the Queensland Ballet as an extra during his final year as a dance student. In *The Sleeping Beauty*, Matthew will be appearing as a suitor, as Aurora's older brother, as a Russian at the wedding and (dressed up in a cape and mask) as one of Carabosse's evil rats. After class is over, Matthew joins the other dancers for a short coffee break, and then the company members reassemble in the studio where Harold Collins, the

Queensland Ballet's artistic director, is waiting for them.

New productions of classical ballets like *The Sleeping Beauty* are not added to a dance company's **repertoire** very often. They are expensive and time-consuming to mount: in fact, by the time the dancers begin rehearsals, at least 18 months work and planning has already gone into the production. Harold, who is also the ballet's **choreographer**, explains the plans that he and David Bell, the director, have made for this production. A ballet like *The Sleeping Beauty*, Harold says, has been produced so many times that many of the dance fans in the audience will have seen it before. The company's challenge is to make an old favorite say something new.

> At least 18 months work and planning has already gone into the production

Over the next six weeks, the dancers settle into a grueling routine of rehearsals. There are three two-hour rehearsals every day; sometimes, there are even separate rehearsals going on in two studios for different parts of the ballet. While Harold Collins is responsible for putting the ballet together, he is helped out at this busy time by two assistants. Benita Whalley, the company's assistant rehearsal director, coaches couples in **pas de deux**, as well as the female dancers who will be dancing the fairies and Princess Aurora. In another part of the building, rehearsal director Anthony Shearsmith is busy rehearsing some very important cast members indeed. Ten young dancers from ballet schools in Queensland and northern New South Wales have been chosen to play the parts of the fairytale children, who are kidnapped by Carabosse and her army of rats. They have beaten over 200 other hopefuls at a tough audition, and will join the rest of the company during the last week of rehearsals.

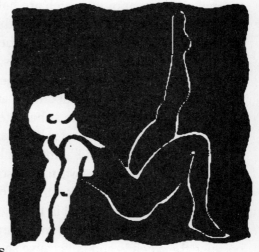

All three casts of principals have to learn their roles together, committing the steps to memory before they can put in the little bit of themselves that will make their performance different. To help them, Harold Collins shows the dancers a videotape of another company's production of the same ballet. Writing down ballets has always been a problem, and today most ballet companies use a special **notation system** called Benesh Notation. Videos are a modern bonus, and luckily Benita Whalley is an expert at reconstructing ballets from tapes. By watching and copying other dancers in the same roles, the company's members can learn some of the steps and get the idea and feel of the different parts.

Of course, there is much more to rehearsing than simply copying. *The Sleeping Beauty* is a very old ballet, and was originally choreographed for a much larger company. This means that some of it will have to be changed or reworked to suit the Queensland Ballet. Harold Collins will also alter parts of the ballet to suit the new direction he and David Bell intend to take with it.

Harold has decided that some parts of Marius Petipa's original choreography — which are both famous and very effective on stage — must be kept. Other sections of the ballet are choreographed by him as the dancers rehearse. Harold works closely with the dancers, putting together steps for the different characters. These must not only be effective to look at: they must tell the audience something about the story, and about the character who is dancing them. For example, a character like Carabosse shows she is wicked and larger than life through lots of dramatic leaps and turns, while her rats swarm and scurry around the stage. Harold also has to take into account the sets and costumes which will be used in the finished production. He spends two days just working with Carabosse's rats, because their heads and tails cause so many problems. If he's not careful in putting together their dances, their heads will fly off and spoil the whole effect!

Rehearsal time for any ballet is always intense and stressful. By the time the six-week rehearsal period is over, the dancers have worn out 200 pairs of shoes, just in practicing. Yet somehow, despite all the stress and anxiety, rehearsing is positive and exciting. For the dancers, this is a time full of discoveries and the thrill of creating something new.

A Dancer's Day

Here is a typical timetable for a dancer's day at the Queensland Ballet, when the company is rehearsing a new production such as *The Sleeping Beauty*.

9.00 A.M.	Arrive at the studio and warm up	1.00 P.M.	Lunch
9.30 A.M.	Daily class	2.15 P.M.	Second rehearsal block
10.45 A.M.	Coffee break	4.00 P.M.	Coffee break
11.00 A.M.	First rehearsal block	4.15 P.M.	Third rehearsal block
		6.00 P.M.	Finish

When the company is giving performances, class starts at 10 A.M., and is followed by a rehearsal which lasts until 2 P.M. The dancers are often back in the theatre by 4.30 or 5 P.M. to give themselves time to get ready before barre practice at 6.45.
The performance starts at 7.30 or 8 and finishes at 10 to 10.30 P.M. — a long and exhausting day.

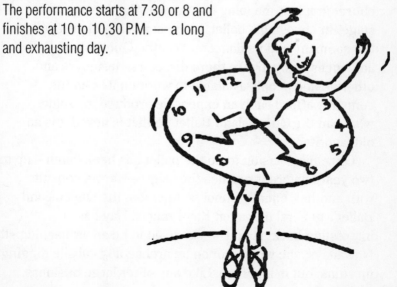

Behind the Scenes

● ● ● ● ● ●

Audience members attending a performance of a ballet like
The Sleeping Beauty usually go to see only one thing — the
dancing. But the Queensland Ballet, like any ballet
company, is made up of more people than dancers. Behind
the scenes are the people who make the ballet happen,
who advise the dancers, who make the production come
alive with lights, music and costume. Without them, there
would be no *Sleeping Beauty* at all.

The most important person in the company is not a
dancer at all, though he used to be one. Harold Collins is
the artistic director, responsible for choosing all the
productions the company mounts. Often he is also the
choreographer, mapping out the way the dancers move on
stage. In choosing a ballet, he must ask whether it will suit
the company and its dancers. Will the Queensland Ballet's
audiences enjoy it? Are there directors, designers and
other skilled people available to work on it? Can the
company afford such an expensive production? And
what can the Queensland Ballet do that is new if it is an
old favorite?

Once his decision to do the ballet has been taken – up to
two years before it reaches the stage – Harold consults
with another, equally important person: the Queensland
Ballet's general manager, Kay Francis. Kay has an
interesting background — she used to be an archaeologist!
Nowadays, she works not on an archaeological site digging
up ruins, but in an office. Like any other large business,

the Queensland Ballet employs people, has budgets and plans to prepare, and products — ballets like *The Sleeping Beauty* — to sell.

Kay is the person who will run the business side of mounting *The Sleeping Beauty*, leaving Harold free to plan the production with the director David Bell, and designer Bill Haycock. Together, the three men decide what direction they would like the ballet to take. David Bell suggests that a new twist to the story would be to show how bleak and sad the world would be without 'Beauty'. Immediately, Bill Haycock

> *how bleak and sad the world would be without 'Beauty'*

latches onto this idea. He says eagerly that he can design sets and costumes to show the world being plunged into winter for a hundred years when Beauty (the Princess Aurora) falls asleep. Harold will be able to show the same thing in his choreography.

Bill Haycock works long and hard designing the costumes and sets. He has to have these ready before the dancers begin rehearsing. As soon as Harold Collins has approved the final designs, Bill gets together with Terry Walduck, the wardrobe supervisor, who has an office and workroom at the far end of the building.

With his team of seven machinists, Terry is the person responsible for making the spectacular costumes worn by the dancers on stage. His work begins about four months before the production is due to open. With Bill Haycock, Terry decides how much money can be spent, and puts together a timetable to make sure everything can be completed for opening night.

The first thing which has to be worked out is how much fabric will be needed. *The Sleeping Beauty* will feature an incredible 94 costumes, so it is important for Terry to get lavish effects for as little money as possible. The rats will need special masks, made out of fiberglass. This work will have to be sent out to a special sculptor. Terry also realizes that because *The Sleeping Beauty* is a nineteenth-century classical ballet, a large part of his budget must be spent on expensive tutus. Tutus cost about $200-300 each, and a good one has up to 16 rows of tulle net. Each tutu uses 50 feet of material — about five times as much as an ordinary woman's dress.

In the production, most roles will be danced by several dancers. Terry cannot afford to make separate costumes for every dancer, so he has to resort to tricks like making false sets of sleeves for people with long arms. He also makes sure that the costumes have big seam allowances so that they can be let out later. But sometimes larger dancers simply have to squeeze into costumes that are too small for them. The dancers don't like this much, because the most important thing for them is that their costume should be comfortable. When the dancers finally get into the costumes the week before the production opens, some people still have problems. Terri-Lee Milne finds Aurora's beautiful cloth-of-gold tutu heavy and uncomfortable because of all the sequins. The rats can't see in their expensive masks. Another company member, dancing the role of Aurora's Italian suitor, absolutely hates the long blond wig he has to wear. Part of Terry's job is to calm people's nerves and try and make sure everybody is happy and comfortable with what they have to wear.

Another item which Terry is responsible for is the pointe shoes. These arrive pink, so if the designer has asked for a different color, they have to be especially painted (for example, the Bluebirds who dance at Aurora's wedding in the Third Act need blue shoes). Since some dancers go through a pair of shoes every night, this is no small job. As Terry says, 'Necessity is the mother of invention, and cheap budgets are the mother of necessity!'

> *Some dancers go through a pair of shoes every night*

No matter how beautifully danced and staged the ballet is, without an audience, all this work is useless. So, like every other big theater, opera or dance company, the Queensland Ballet employs a special person to promote it: the marketing manager, Jane Murphy. Jane's job is to make sure people hear about the Queensland Ballet, and buy tickets to the company's performances. For *The Sleeping Beauty*, Jane has arranged a subscription offer, television advertisement, newspaper ads and brochures, which will be put in 35,000 mailboxes around Brisbane. She has helped a graphic artist design the production's program and a beautiful rose-colored poster of Terri-Lee Milne as Aurora. To do all this, she has been given a budget of $30,000. This sounds like a lot of money, but a single newspaper ad can cost around $1000, so Jane has to spend it very carefully. (Big shows like *Cats* or *The Phantom of the Opera* will easily spend ten times this amount.)

Luckily, *The Sleeping Beauty* is a popular ballet. By the time it is due to open, Jane's work has paid off, and most of the tickets have been sold. The money will help pay for this, and other Queensland Ballet productions. But until it is seen on stage, nobody knows whether *The Sleeping Beauty* will be an artistic success as well.

Opening night is still to come....

Dancers in the Wings:
The Queensland Dance School of Excellence

Every morning at 8 A.M. students of the Queensland Dance School of Excellence arrive at the Thomas Dixon Centre, home of the Queensland Ballet. They spend four hours studying different types of dance, perhaps working with a choreographer or rehearsing for one of the many performances the school gives throughout the year. Then, at 1 P.M. a bus arrives and takes them across the river to the Kelvin Grove High School for three hours of ordinary schoolwork. At the end of twelfth grade, graduates of the Q.D.S.E. will have not only a diploma in dancing, but a full Senior Certificate.

Some students don't make it through to the end

Entry into the course is difficult, as only 25 people can be taken on each year. Students are expected to have finished tenth grade at school, and must pass a tough audition, as well as a personal interview in the company of their parents. The course itself is very demanding, and some students don't make it through to the end. Although people who are accepted into the school are usually highly dedicated, some of them just can't handle the heavy workload of tiring dance training and difficult schoolwork. Angus Lugsdin, the school co-ordinator, says that some people — particularly girls who have romantic dreams of being ballerinas — find the course is not what they thought. However, students who do finish the course at least have the option of using their Senior marks to go to university, or into other interesting jobs.

Q.D.S.E. students Trisha Shorten and Michael Kopp have both wanted to be dancers since they were small. They agree that being able to combine dance training with going to an ordinary school is a great opportunity, though Trisha says, 'It's tough doing the two together.' Trisha gets up every day at 6 A.M. and doesn't finish working until 6 P.M. (Some students even do extra dance training in the evenings, but Trisha says she's too tired.) Both Trisha and Michael have had to leave home to do the Q.D.S.E. course. Michael, from Hervey Bay in Queensland, boards with friends, but Trisha, who comes from Sydney, lives in a hostel with 16 other girls. 'I was very homesick the first term,' she says, 'but you get used to it.'

For those who finish and decide to make dance their career, there are a number of exciting options. Occasionally, an exceptional student like Matthew Thomson will go straight into the Queensland Ballet or another dance company. Others will go on to further dance studies. Trisha Shorten would like to travel overseas, but doesn't really care where she goes as long as she can dance. 'For me, dancing is a way of expressing myself,' she says. 'You can tell whether someone loves to dance by the expression on their face.'

The Story of The Sleeping Beauty

● ● ● ● ● ●

The ballet begins with a **Prologue**. In Fairytale Land, the King and Queen are delighted by the birth of a Princess – Aurora. They invite everyone to come and see their new daughter, including all the children from the fairytales, and seven fairies. The fairies bring magic gifts – beauty, goodness, grace, eloquence, energy and wisdom. But suddenly the sky darkens. Hideous rats flood into the celebration and the wicked fairy Carabosse appears – uninvited – to curse the little Princess. Aurora, she declares, will die on her sixteenth birthday.

Everyone is horrified. Then the Lilac Fairy steps forward. Although she cannot stop the curse, her magic can soften its effect. Instead of dying, the Princess will fall into a deep sleep, from which she can only be awakened by a kiss from her true love.

Carabosse flees – but not before ordering her rats to steal all the fairytale children and carry them away to her enchanted kingdom.

In **Act One**, we move on to Aurora's sixteenth birthday. The Princess is lonely and unhappy. Her parents wish her to marry, and bring four handsome young men for her to choose a husband from. Aurora rejects all of them. While she is alone, a mysterious figure appears...

The stranger gives Aurora a birthday kiss, and suddenly the Princess grows faint. She is dying! The mysterious figure reveals herself as Carabosse. But the Lilac Fairy arrives to cast a spell of her own, and instead of dying Aurora falls into a deep, deep sleep.

Many years pass. When **Act Two** opens, it is the dead of winter. Pursued by a magic troop of leaden soldiers, a handsome prince appears out of the darkness. Recognizing Aurora's true love, the Lilac Fairy shows the young man a vision of the sleeping princess. The prince dances with the vision, and when it fades, begs the Fairy to show him where the beautiful young woman lies.

The Prince is guided through Carabosse's magic world, past the rats and the captive fairytale children, to the place where Aurora lies, asleep in a bed of flowers. He kisses her gently on the lips and she wakes. At first Aurora is frightened, but the Prince gains her trust, and soon she is as charmed by him as he is by her. They dance, and their love breaks the spell. As the sun comes up, the captive children are released.

In **Act Three** Aurora is reunited with the fairytale characters of her childhood. She introduces her friends to the Prince, and they dance to celebrate her return as everyone prepares to live happily ever after...

The Characters

Sometimes being a successful dancer is as much about knowing how to act as knowing how to dance! Here, three principal dancers talk about the way they saw their character in *The Sleeping Beauty*.

Terri-Lee Milne on the Princess Aurora

'The role of Sleeping Beauty is technically demanding, but she's really quite a straightforward person. It's not like dancing Giselle, where you have to go mad! In our production she's a little bit frustrated — her parents have smothered her with love, trying to make things up to her because of the terrible spell which has been placed on her. Aurora rebels against this: she's a typical teenager in a lot of ways.'

Graham Fletcher on the Prince

'Actually, the Prince is a bit of a "nothing" character — he's just Prince Charming, he's "nice". He's very much second in line, because the whole story revolves around Beauty. She's the important one.

'Also, the Prince doesn't come into the ballet until the second act, which can be a bit of an extra challenge. You have to sit around for about an hour and a half, which can make you quite nervous.'

Michelle Giammichele on Carabosse

'Carabosse drips evil: she's just a spiteful person, and vain. Every scene she's in is very dramatic. Harold [the choreographer] did a brilliant job of my character: it was full of turns and grand gestures and leaps. It was very demanding to dance, because before you come on stage you have to be really psyched up to make a big impact: also danced the Princess on alternative nights, so I went from one extreme to the other.'

Performance!

● ● ● ● ● ●

The week leading up to the opening night of *The Sleeping Beauty* is the tensest and busiest of all. Everyone — artistic director, dancers, lighting designer, director — is fighting for precious last-minute opportunities to make everything perfect for the first performance. Yet it is now, in the midst of all the bustle and confusion, that the company must pull together and more than ever work as a team.

The Thursday of the week before the ballet opens begins with an exciting and nerve-wracking moment: one that tells the dancers once and for all that opening night is just around the corner. The costumes — beautiful jeweled tutus in rainbow shades, princely capes, comical rats' tails and masks — arrive from Terry Walduck's workshop. Dance students dream of wearing such gorgeous clothes, but for Terri-Lee Milne and the rest of the company the costumes are actually a nuisance. All through the rehearsal period, they have been dancing in their old, comfortable practice clothes. As soon as they put on the stiff, formal costumes, everything feels different, and all sorts of little things start going wrong.

> As soon as they put on the stiff, formal costumes, all sorts of things start going wrong

The first time Carabosse's army of rats wear their costumes to dance, rat number 2 stands on rat number 3's tail, and all the rats end up in a heap on the ground. When the company is rehearsing the second act, one of the fairies is lifted up into the air by her partner, and her tutu comes apart at the waist. The bottom half stays on the ground, the top half stays on the dancer! Of course, everybody bursts out laughing, the rehearsal grinds to a halt, and the offending tutu is whisked back to Terry's workshop for repairs. But the moment passes quickly, and before long everyone is hard at work again. Gradually, costumes and steps come together, and the ballet starts looking a little more like the spectacular performance that will soon be seen on stage.

While the dancers are getting used to their costumes, in another part of the Thomas Dixon Centre a different type of rehearsal is getting under way. In its studios, the Queensland Philharmonic Orchestra has started practicing the famous Tchaikovsky music which it will play at the performances of the ballet. Until now the dancers have been rehearsing to a piano, or tapes of other orchestras playing the music. This may seem a late time for the musicians to become involved, but because an orchestra is very expensive to run (and all the musicians have to be paid for rehearsal time), no dance company will rehearse with one until it is absolutely necessary.

By now it is Monday morning. There are only three days left until opening night.

While the dancers and orchestra rehearse separately at the Thomas Dixon Centre, at the Suncorp Theatre members of the stage crew have taken over. Like an army of ants, they swarm backstage putting together *The Sleeping Beauty*'s sets. Ballet sets have to be designed very carefully, so the scenery doesn't get in the way of the dancers. Bill Haycock, the designer, has looked after this –

and then let his imagination run riot. He has designed sets which are strange and magical, even surreal — including, amongst other props, two huge synthetic heads. (Later, one night during an interstate tour, one of the heads catches fire in the middle of Aurora's birthday party! It is up to Anthony Shearsmith, dancing the King, to bravely whip it off the stage where there is a fire

> *One of the heads catches fire in the middle of Aurora's birthday party!*

extinguisher.) Specialist members of the crew also set to work rigging up thousands of dollars worth of lighting equipment. Lighting designer David Whitworth is busy planning the lighting that will create special moods and effects on stage, and spotlight the dancers' performances and costumes.

Finally, on Wednesday, the day before the ballet opens, there is a **dress rehearsal** in the theater. Only now, less than 48 hours before the first performance, does everything — sets, costumes, lighting, dancers and orchestra — come together for the first time.

The first dress rehearsal always uses the first cast, so Terri-Lee Milne is dancing Aurora. But she is back again early on Thursday — the morning of opening night —for a second dress rehearsal, because the second cast principals must also be given the chance to rehearse. Terri-Lee dances her smaller roles of a fairy and the Prince's sister, then goes home to prepare for the big evening's work ahead. She says that she is more excited than nervous about the evening's performance. Nevertheless, most of the dancers are starting to feel jittery, and everyone involved is tense. Until the production has been tested in front of an audience, no one can be sure whether the choreography and the directors' ideas have worked. In just a few hours time, they will know whether all their hard work has paid off.

The dancers begin to arrive at the theater late in the afternoon. Each dancer has to do his or her own hair and makeup, so their arrival time partly depends on how complicated this is. All of them are terribly excited — and nervous about the coming performance. Stage fright and first-night nerves are something all dancers have to deal with, and each member of the company has developed a different way of coping. Michelle Giammichele says that she likes to be by herself, so that there will be no distractions and she can focus everything on her dancing. Graham Fletcher, who will be taking the role of the Prince, believes that the best thing to do is to get out on stage as soon as possible and start dancing. Tonight, unfortunately, he will not be able to do this. His character does not appear until Act Two: halfway through the ballet. For the first hour and a half, he will be watching the other dancers from the wings.

Three-quarters of an hour before the performance

starts, there is barre practice. The dancers do exercises to warm up their bodies for the performance – while outside, the first members of the audience are beginning to arrive. They buy programs and drinks, and stand around chatting. Among them are the **dance critics** who will write about the performance in newspapers. If their reports of *The Sleeping Beauty* are favorable, more people will come, both to performances in Brisbane and to the interstate tours which are soon to follow.

In the orchestra pit, members of the Queensland Philharmonic are tuning up in preparation for their performance. At 7.50 P.M. a bell starts ringing in the theatre foyer, telling audience members the ballet is about to begin. Backstage, the dancers are waiting in the wings, anxiously checking their costumes, doing a few last-minute stretching exercises, and running through in their mind any difficult sequences in the choreography. Anthony Shearsmith speaks a few words of encouragement to the children he has coached, who are about to make their debut as Aurora's fairytale playmates.

Last-minute stretching exercises

The dancers who will enter first take up their positions. There is a little ripple of applause as the conductor enters, and the orchestra strikes up the overture. On stage, the lights come up and ...

Two hours later, exhausted and smiling, the dancers take their last curtain call, and exit backstage. They are followed by the sound of the audience's applause. Aurora has been bewitched by Carabosse, and woken up by her prince; and everyone has danced joyfully at their wedding. Everything about the ballet has gone exactly according to plan.

Outside, the dance critics disappear with their notebooks to write up an article for Saturday morning's review column. Harold Collins, who has been watching the performance carefully, hurries backstage to congratulate the dancers, and give them hints on how to improve their next performance. The fairytale children from the local dance schools are reunited with their proud parents. Friends and well-wishers arrive with congratulations. In the dressing rooms, the dancers change out of their costumes and take off their makeup so they can celebrate the birth of the Queensland Ballet's latest production.

Meanwhile, happy audience members are spilling out onto the sidewalk, and the theater staff are beginning to close up the building. The first performance is over.

The Sleeping Beauty is a success.

Anna's Sleeping Beauty

One of the most famous dancers in history, Anna Pavlova, was introduced to ballet as a small girl, when her mother took her to see a performance of *The Sleeping Beauty*.

Anna's mother was a widow, and very poor. Yet somehow she scraped enough money together to buy two tickets in the upper balcony of the Maryinski Theatre to give her daughter a Christmas treat. In later life, Anna remembered being driven to the theatre in a sleigh through the snow-filled streets of St. Petersburg. When she asked where they were headed, her mother replied that they were going 'to the country of the fairies'.

Together Anna and her mother climbed the stairs to the upper balcony: the very cheapest seats in the theatre. The lights dimmed. As soon as the music started to play, young Anna began to tremble. From that night on, she wrote, 'I knew I must give the rest of my life to dancing'. Her mother was very unhappy that her delicate daughter wanted to enter such a difficult profession, but Anna was determined, even though everybody said she was far too frail to cope with a ballerina's difficult training.

Two years later, at the age of 10, Anna Pavlova entered the Imperial Ballet School. At 18, she graduated and became a member of the same ballet company she had seen at the Maryinski Theatre as a little girl. And years later, when she was a famous ballerina touring the world and enchanting millions of people, she danced the role of the Sleeping Beauty herself.

Star Spots: Some Famous Dancers

The Little Hunchback: Marie Taglioni

●●●●●●●

Dancers usually begin their training when they are children. By starting young, a dancer can develop a supple and muscular body, able to take the terrible strain of performing night after night. Yet Marie Taglioni, who is today remembered as one of the greatest ballerinas in history, not only wasted the opportunities she was given as a child — she was told by her teacher she had no talent! Marie Taglioni's late start and dazzling career is one of the great success stories of ballet. Like the ugly duckling in the fairy story, the plain little girl with the rounded shoulders grew up to be a graceful swan.

Marie Taglioni was born in Stockholm in 1804. Her mother was Swedish, and her Italian father, Philippe or Filippo, was a successful choreographer and ballet master. Soon after Marie was born, the Taglioni family moved to Vienna, where Filippo worked at the court theater for the Austrian Emperor himself. Filippo came from a family of dancers, and naturally he expected that both Marie and her young brother Paul would follow in the family tradition.

At that time Paris was the world center of ballet training. When Marie was old enough to start studying ballet seriously, her father decided to send her there. There was only one problem. Young Marie absolutely hated dancing. She was thin, plain, had very long arms and legs, and stooped so badly that her Parisian ballet teacher is supposed to have called her a little hunchback! Perhaps because she was so badly teased, Marie made sure she dodged her ballet lessons whenever she could. Because she did no practice, she made hardly any progress. Her teacher even told her mother Sophie she would be better off learning to be a dressmaker.

Young Marie absolutely hated dancing

Marie's father Filippo knew nothing of this. Far away in Austria, he was busy making plans for his daughter's **debut**. In fact, he was so confident in Marie's ability he was even putting together a ballet for the occasion — and casting her in the leading role! Most young dancers would have been thrilled by this exciting news, but when she received her father's letter, 17-year-old Marie was horrified. She knew her dancing was terrible. If she made her debut now, she would not only disappoint her father, she would probably be booed off the stage.

Late in 1821 Marie, her mother and younger brother set off for distant Vienna. In the few months before her departure Marie had practiced doubly hard to make up for her years of laziness, but her efforts were not enough. When Filippo saw her dance, he was aghast. How could Marie's dancing be so bad, when he had received such glowing accounts of her progress? It turned out that Sophie had been trying to protect her daughter from Filippo's anger by sending false reports about her progress. Filippo told Marie firmly that her days of laziness were over. Her debut could not be cancelled, so from now on she must work until she was ready to drop.

If Marie had worked at her lessons when she was in Paris, she would have had years to build up her strength, fitness and technique. Instead she had only a couple of months. Every day for six hours she would practice the grueling exercises her father had devised for her, until she was dripping with perspiration and almost weeping with the pain of her aching muscles. Sometimes, she nearly fainted with exhaustion. But despite what her Paris teacher had said, Marie Taglioni was a very talented dancer. Gradually, her hard work started to pay off.

The day of the debut arrived. Although she was terribly nervous, Marie had been well prepared by her father. She danced beautifully, and her performance was acclaimed as a triumph. Everyone who saw her commented on her grace and lightness, and — amazingly for those days — no one even noticed how plain she was. In fact, Marie's 'ugly' long arms and legs soon became her greatest asset. Her long legs helped her to leap effortlessly across the stage, landing as softly as a fairy. And other dancers were soon copying the graceful way she folded her arms across her chest — even though she started doing this to hide the length of her arms.

Another thing Marie Taglioni is often reported to have invented is dancing *sur les pointes* ('on the points', or toes). Today, we take this sort of dancing for granted, but when Marie began her career it was still quite uncommon. Dancers were not trained for it, and they also had to do it without the hard 'toe shoes' that support the modern dancer's feet. In fact, Marie Taglioni was not the first dancer to dance on pointe. However, she was certainly one of the first to make it popular, and she also helped establish the technique needed to do it.

Filippo Taglioni soon realized that his daughter was particularly good at dancing fairies and spirits. In fact, when dancing these roles she almost seemed to float across the stage. He decided to put together a ballet especially for Marie where she could show off these abilities. The ballet was called *La Sylphide*, and was about the love of a young Scotsman for a beautiful fairy. It was a huge hit, and made Marie extremely famous. In her soft white dress and tiny wings Marie almost seemed to fly (at one stage, helped by a special harness and flying wires, she actually did). Nowadays *La Sylphide* is not often performed, but in its day it was tremendously important, and it is still known as the first true 'Romantic' ballet. ('Romantic' here does not mean a love story, but a story about fantastic, magical or exotic places and people. Romantic ballets often featured fairies, curses and ghosts.)

Romantic dance became a craze. Soon every other ballet was a *ballet blanc* (white ballet), with long lines of girls in floaty white dresses. (The only people to lose out were the poor male dancers, who spent the next 100 years or so carrying sylphs and fairies around the stage.) Not everyone admired the new style of dancing, however, and not all dancers were good at it. In later years an unofficial 'war' was waged between Marie and a fiery young dancer called Fanny Elssler. Fanny Elssler specialized in lively, exotic dances, and unlike Marie she was very beautiful. Supporters of the two dancers would go to the rival's performances and boo them loudly. Sometimes there would even be brawls! Descriptions of these performances make them sound more like modern football matches than a night at the theater.

> **More like modern football matches than a night at the theater**

Marie Taglioni retired from dancing in 1848, when she was 44. In real life, she was a quiet, shy woman with simple tastes. Her private life was very unhappy. She married a French aristocrat who spent all her earnings and then deserted her; she fell in love with another man, but he died. Later, a violent revolution shook France, and she was forced to move to Italy, leaving many of her possessions behind.

Although she had made a fortune from her dancing, Marie lost most of her money. But she never lost the love of ballet that her father Filippo had given her when she was an unwilling, 'untalented' teenager. Marie knew that without Filippo's help she would never have succeeded as a dancer; she also knew that her own experience would now be invaluable to others. Marie Taglioni, one of history's most famous ballerinas, spent her later years teaching and coaching younger dancers — the way her father had once coached her.

The Butterfly

One of the most tragic stories in the history of ballet is that of Emma Livry. Beautiful and talented, Emma was a protégé of Marie Taglioni. Marie Taglioni coached her, and even choreographed a ballet for her. It was called *Le Papillon* — the Butterfly — and told the story of a beautiful moth which flew into a candle flame and was burned to death.

In the mid-nineteenth century, most theaters had gas footlights. The presence of naked flames so close to the people on stage was dangerous, and a law was passed ordering all costumes to be specially fire-proofed. But Emma Livry thought her fire-proofed costume was heavy and ugly, and not as effective as the floating butterfly skirts she was used to. She refused to wear it. One night, while rehearsing at the Paris Opera House, her costume brushed against a footlight. In a flash, the ballerina's beautiful muslin skirt went up in flames.

Immediately, a theater worker threw a blanket over the screaming dancer. The fire was extinguished — but not before Emma had been horribly burned from head to foot. She died eight months later, in excruciating agony, after a brilliant career of just four years. She was only 20. Like the butterfly in her famous ballet, Emma Livry had literally danced too close to the flame...

Isadora Duncan

● ● ● ● ● ●

Today, 'modern dance' is very popular. Many dancers specialize in this exciting and dynamic form of dance, and people all over the world go to see new productions by famous modern dance companies. One of the most important pioneers of modern dance was a remarkable woman who lived and worked in the early years of this century. For Isadora Duncan, it was impossible to live without dancing. The story of her passionate ideals and her sad life has inspired other dancers to the present day.

Angela Isadora Duncan was born in San Francisco in about 1877 or 1878. Her father was Scottish, her mother a proud, wild Irish music teacher who helped develop in young Isadora a lifelong love of music. When she was quite a small girl, her father walked out. The family had little money and few possessions, and was constantly on the move. For the rest of her life, Isadora had trouble putting down roots. She was always restlessly traveling from place to place, country to country, and it was unusual for her to settle down anywhere for more than year or so.

> **Isadora had trouble putting down roots**

Eventually, Isadora's parents were divorced. Isadora had been deeply hurt by their unhappy marriage and grew up insisting that women should be free to do whatever they wanted. She herself knew exactly what she wanted to do — dance. Although she seems to have had few proper lessons, as a little girl Isadora was constantly dancing, and encouraging her friends to dance too. When she was a teenager, the Duncan family moved to Chicago and later New York, so she could pursue her career on the stage.

In New York, Isadora Duncan danced in theaters and in the music halls that were popular at the time. Isadora thought this type of dancing was ugly and pointless, but three years of it allowed her to save up just enough money to travel to Europe on a cattle boat. In London, she danced in the theater, and privately at parties for rich and famous people. Already her ideas about dancing were taking shape. She visited museums where she studied sculptures and vase paintings of dancers from ancient Greece. Isadora loved the simplicity of the Grecian clothes, the dancers' bare feet, and their natural-looking movements, and she adopted all these things into her own unique style of dance. For several years, she performed in cities across Europe. Then finally, in 1904, she had her breakthrough. The Urania theatre in Budapest, Hungary, contracted the talented auburn-haired dancer to appear there for a month. From the moment she stepped on stage in her simple white tunic, Isadora Duncan was a sensation.

Isadora's Hungarian success gave her money, and a little security. She decided it was time to go back to the roots of dance — to Greece itself. In Athens, Isadora climbed the Acropolis at dawn to visit the famous ancient temple known as the Parthenon and was so overcome by the experience that she began dancing then and there! Isadora decided to stay in Greece, and she and her family began building a home which they designed to resemble an ancient Grecian palace. But by the time the house was completed, the restless Isadora was ready to move on. She had a mission to take her extraordinary form of dance to the outside world. This was something she could only accomplish by performing.

Isadora Duncan's performances were simple, but effective. Onto a bare stage, backed by plain blue curtains, she would emerge barefoot in her Grecian tunic. Her movements were nothing like the leaps and poses which audiences were used to in ballet. In fact, they were ordinary, everyday movements, made special by the dancer's own grace and emotion. Isadora was always watching people (including herself) to see how they reacted to the outside world. When she wanted to show sadness in her dancing, she looked at a sad person, saw how they moved, and copied that movement.

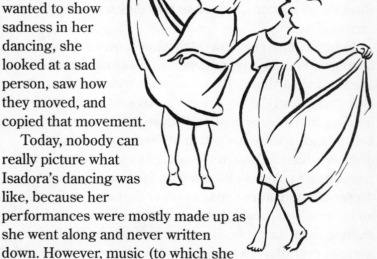

Today, nobody can really picture what Isadora's dancing was like, because her performances were mostly made up as she went along and never written down. However, music (to which she was extremely sensitive) was always an important part.

Isadora also knew how to sway an audience's emotions. In Paris at the height of World War I, while the French army and their allies were fighting to drive the Germans out of France, she gave a passionate performance to music of the French national anthem, *La Marseillaise*, which brought everyone cheering to their feet.

Unlike many dancers, whose only ambition was to make a career on the stage, Isadora loved to dance in temples, churches, gardens — in fact, anywhere. Her 'theory' of dancing was quite simple. She recognized that even the tiniest children will wave their hands and sway about to music if they get the opportunity, and that wanting to dance is a natural part of being human — like eating or sleeping. (Isadora claimed she danced in her mother's womb!) Isadora Duncan believed that the desire to dance came from a person's soul, and that it was a way for everyone to show their emotions, as well as how they felt about their surroundings.

In her lifetime, Isadora established dance schools in Germany, France, and in Russia. Her lessons were nothing like the ones ordinary dance students were used to. Isadora Duncan did not believe in rules or rigid methods of training, and she particularly despised the way young ballet dancers were hedged in by teachers wanting to discipline them. The aim of her classes was to teach her pupils how to express themselves. Isadora's students dressed in miniature versions of her famous Grecian tunic, and she helped them grow strong enough for dancing by making them do gymnastics. She also taught them to use normal, everyday movements like running and jumping in their dancing.

Partly because her views and way of life were so extreme compared to those of other people of her time, Isadora Duncan had a very unhappy life. As a beautiful, talented woman, she had many admirers and lovers, but sooner or later most of these relationships went wrong. In 1913, her two children, Deirdre and Patrick, were killed in a terrible accident. They were sitting in a parked car with their nurse by the River Seine in Paris. The brakes failed, the car plunged down an embankment into the river, and both the children and their nurse were trapped inside and drowned. Deirdre was six, and baby Patrick was only two.

Isadora Duncan never recovered from this tragedy. The memory of her dead children haunted her for the rest of her life. She began to drink too much, and even thought about committing suicide. Only her dancing kept her going. A year after Deirdre and Patrick died, she had a third baby, but this little boy lived only for a few hours. Years afterwards, Isadora wrote that she could still barely look at a child without bursting into tears.

Worse was to come. In 1921, excited by the communist revolution which had been happening in Russia, Isadora and her adopted daughter Irma traveled to Moscow to dance and teach. Here, she fell madly in love with a young Russian poet, Sergei Esenin, whose angelic face and golden curls reminded her of her lost baby, Patrick. They married, but while Sergei looked like an angel with his golden hair, he treated his wife cruelly, ordered her around, and sometimes even beat her.

By now Isadora Duncan was a plump, middle-aged

> She fell madly in love with a young Russian poet

woman with dyed red hair; but her dancing still thrilled audiences wherever she performed. Esenin became jealous of her success. He stole from her, spent her money, and threatened to kill her. Eventually, after a stormy scene in Paris where he completely wrecked their hotel room, he became so mentally unstable that the couple separated. Back in Moscow in late 1925, Esenin cut open a vein in his wrist and wrote a last poem in his own blood. The next day, he committed suicide by hanging himself.

Isadora was numbed and saddened by her husband's death. Her life had become so awful that death now seemed the only escape. She danced in Paris on 8 July 1927, and set off soon afterwards for Nice in southern France. On the evening of 14 September, a young man came to pick her up for a drive in his open sports car. Dressed in her favorite red shawl, which she wore to perform her famous dance *La Marseillaise*, Isadora said goodbye to her friends in French : *'Adieu mes amis. Je vais à la gloire.'* ('Goodbye my friends. I am heading for glory.') She climbed into the car, and the driver set off. Her good friend, Mary Desti, described what happened next:

The car started slowly, it had hardly gone ten yards, when I noticed the fringe of her shawl, like a streak of blood, hanging behind, dragging in the dirt...Suddenly, the car stopped...as Isadora threw her shawl around her neck and across her shoulder, the heavy fringe, hanging down behind, had caught in the rear wheel...The very first revolution of the wheel had broken her neck...

Isadora Duncan's sad, wonderful, tragic life was over. The world of dance would never be quite the same.

The Little Brother: Fred Astaire

● ● ● ● ● ●

Many dancers start their careers because there are other dancers in the family — usually a mother or father. But Fred Astaire, the most famous dancing movie star of all time, made a more unusual start to his career — tagging along behind an older sister!

Fred Astaire was born Frederick Austerlitz in Omaha, Nebraska, in 1899. His elder sister, Adele, was 18 months older than he, and by the time Fred was toddling she was already showing a remarkable talent for dancing. Then, in 1904, disaster struck the family. Fred's father lost his job. What should they do? The solution was obvious. They would go to New York, center of the American entertainment industry, and Adele would go on the stage.

Leaving Mr. Austerlitz in Omaha to look for work, the family moved to New York. Here it was decided that young Fred should go to dancing lessons as well. He too was showing signs of ability, and besides, it would be easier for Adele to get work if she already had a partner. Soon the talented duo were getting vaudeville work under a new, more glamorous name – 'Astaire'. But behind the scenes, the young stars were just a normal brother and sister. Fred used to pray at night that God would turn his sister into a

> *Fred used to pray that God would turn his sister into a boy*

boy, while Adele wished her brother was a sweet little girl. Once, she tried to tie a pink bow in Fred's hair — and received a punch in the eye for her pains!

By the time their teens ended, Adele and Fred were big Broadway stars. They toured England a number of times, where the Prince of Wales attended one of their shows ten times! About this time, the first talking movie, *The Jazz Singer*, was shown in America. Fred and Adele were doubtful whether the craze for 'talkies' would last, but they did take a screen test for Paramount, one of the big film studios. Although the studio quite liked Adele — she was still the real star — they were not so impressed with Fred, and told the couple they had no future in the movies. In any case, the long partnership of brother and sister was about to be broken up. Adele had met and fallen in love with a handsome young Englishman, Lord Charles Cavendish, and in 1932 she announced that she was going to marry him and live in England.

For the first time in his life, Fred Astaire was without a dancing partner. He tried dancing with other women, but none of them measured up to the brilliant Adele. Then, in 1933, he decided to take the plunge and move to Hollywood. Since the release of *The Jazz Singer* only six years before, the new 'talkies' had taken the public by storm. For people like Fred, this was good news. For the first time, movies could include not only dialogue but music, singing — and dancing.

Although Fred was a big star on the stage, it was by no means certain that he would be successful on the screen. One studio executive even wrote a report on his screen test which read: 'Can't act. Slightly bald. Also dances'! His first screen role (in an MGM film called *Dancing Lady*) was quite a small one, but soon he was cast in another movie called *Flying Down to Rio*. It was about a man who follows his girlfriend to Brazil, and included an amazing flying sequence with hundreds of chorus girls doing high-kicks on the wings of biplanes! In the film, Fred found himself playing opposite a talented and very professional young dancer called Ginger Rogers. Could it be that he had found a replacement for Adele?

Flying Down to Rio was a hit. Although they were not supposed to be the movie's stars, Fred and Ginger stole the show. Their big dance act, 'The Carioca', was everybody's favorite scene, and before long Fred and Ginger found themselves starring in a movie of their own. This was also a box-office smash, and over the next few years they made a series of movies including *Night and Day*, *Carefree* and *Top Hat*. In this movie, Fred did his famous 'machine gun' dance. Dressed in his elegant trademark evening suit, he 'shot' chorus dancers with his walking cane as he danced past them. He also had a famous argument with Ginger Rogers.

Like many actresses, Ginger loved beautiful clothes, and for the song 'Dancing Cheek to Cheek' she decided to wear a glamorous ball gown, sewn from top to bottom with ostrich feathers. Unfortunately, as soon as she started dancing, all the feathers flew off the dress — straight into Fred's nose and eyes! After an hour's sneezing and tripping, Fred lost his temper. He started calling Ginger 'Feathers' and even sang a rude version of the song from the side of the set. Things were only patched up when the costume designer promised to sit up all night sewing every feather individually in place. But Ginger kept her dress, and for the rest of her career, she maintained it was the prettiest she ever wore.

Normally, Fred and Ginger got on quite well together. However, their famous partnership was to last only six years. Ginger knew that a dancer's working life was often a short one, and was anxious to establish herself as a serious actress. And after losing Adele, Fred was nervous about becoming too closely associated with another dancer. In 1939, they made their last movie together, and Fred went on to star opposite many other famous actresses including Rita Hayworth, Cyd Charisse and Ava Gardner. In his late fifties, he was still dancing. Suave, sophisticated and a superb dancer, he became a hero to people all over the world.

In later life, Fred Astaire went on to a number of serious acting roles, and was even nominated for an Academy Award. But today, he is chiefly remembered for his films with Ginger Rogers, and for the enormous influence he had on dance in the movies. Fred realized that dancing in movies was very different to dancing on stage, and that it

Terri-Lee Milne and Graham Fletcher in the Queensland Ballet's
Sleeping Beauty

Above: The wardrobe department of the Queensland Ballet
Below: Members of the Rippon Lea Renaissance Dancers of Melbourne

Above: Brisbane belly dancer Yani
Below: Doing the limbo at Ripponlea Primary School dance

Anna Pavlova leaving Waterloo station for America

was possible to do things on film which could never be done live. Yet his stage experience also taught him that above all the dance had to flow. He particularly hated trick photography, cutting in and out to the dancers' feet, which he thought interrupted the smoothness of the act, and he insisted that his dances be filmed with as few interruptions as possible. Fred was also an innovative choreographer. He and Ginger would dance effortlessly up and down staircases. over tables, chairs, even, in one movie, across a giant map of the United States. To achieve this effect, he would sometimes shoot the same scene over and over again. In one movie, *Swing Time*, he did 47 takes of a single dance, making Ginger Rogers dance until her feet bled!

He made Ginger Rogers dance until her feet bled!

Fred Astaire had a long, active and happy life. Unlike many Hollywood stars, he preferred to live quietly, playing golf, going to the races, and spending time with his family (he was happily married twice). Most importantly, he always stayed young at heart: at the age of 86, he broke his wrist riding on a skateboard! Perhaps the fact that this happiness showed in his dancing, and made millions of other people happy all over the world, is the real secret of his success.

A One-Legged Dancer . . .

In nineteenth-century Australia, it was difficult to train as a dancer. Most of the performers on Australian stages were visitors from overseas — and one of the strangest acts to tour was Signor Donato, the one-legged dancer! While amazed audiences looked on, Signor Donato performed a polka, a hornpipe and a cloak dance, dressed as a Spanish matador. He also performed a *pas de deux* with a woman dancer, and in all, toured the country for nearly six months. Following his performances in Brisbane, a local critic wrote that he danced better on one leg than most people could on two.

Not everyone was quite so impressed. When Donato appeared in Sydney, a local comedian's response was to go one better and bill himself as 'Signor Tomato the three-legged dancer'!

...and a Lady with a Whip

A more famous visitor to nineteenth-century Australia was Lola Montes. Although her name sounds Spanish, Lola Montes was actually Irish. Most historians agree she probably wasn't much of a dancer. However, Lola was spectacularly beautiful, and had a powerful personality which certainly made an impression on her audiences.

Lola Montes first performed in Australia in Sydney, in 1855. She danced several 'Spanish' dances; in her most famous one, the 'Spider Dance', she pretended a spider had crawled up her skirts! The chief appeal of the dance was no doubt Lola's shapely legs. In the nineteenth century, all women wore long, floor-length skirts, but Lola's were up around her knees. When she visited Melbourne, the dance was considered so indecent that half her performances had to be cancelled, because of the complaints!

Half her performances had to be cancelled

However, the most famous incident of Lola Montes' Australian tour occurred in Ballarat. In those days, Ballarat was a mining town, and very rough. The men who had gone there to work on the goldfields thought Lola's performances were wonderful, and showered her with gold nuggets whenever she went on stage. Only one man, Henry Seekamp, dared to disagree. He published an article in his newspaper, the *Ballarat Times*, which said very uncomplimentary things about her indeed.

Lola determined to get her revenge.When she heard her enemy was drinking in the bar of the hotel where she was staying, she stormed into the bar and started slashing at him wildly with a whip. Seekamp fought back, and soon the two were engaged in a regular brawl, which had to be broken up by the other customers. But Lola was generally regarded as the winner, and her fiery visit to Ballarat has passed into Australian folklore.

A Perfect Partnership: Fonteyn and Nureyev

● ● ● ● ● ●

It is not as easy for two dancers to dance together successfully as people might think. Often a difference of technique, or even a personality clash, gets in the way of the partnership. But when dancers are perfectly partnered, the results can be very exciting.

In 1961, the English ballerina Margot Fonteyn was in her early forties. She had reached the very top of her profession, and was loved by audiences everywhere for her grace and elegance. At her age, most dancers would be beginning to think of retiring, perhaps going on to jobs in teaching or management. Then a spectacular new dancer — young enough to be her son — arrived in Western Europe from Russia, and the course of Margot Fonteyn's career completely changed.

The young dancer was Rudolf Nureyev, a Tartar from the distant Ural Mountains, and a rising star in Russia's famous Kirov Ballet. At this time, relations between the Western world and communist-run Russia (then part of the Soviet Union) were very bad. Both sides were deeply suspicious of each other, and although no war ever broke out, crossing from one side to the other was almost impossible.

As a star dancer with the Kirov Ballet, Rudolf Nureyev was one of the few people lucky enough to be allowed to leave the Soviet Union. Although his life as a dancer was privileged by Russian standards, he hated the constant rules and restrictions which were placed on him by the government. He knew that life in the West would offer far more opportunities to a talented, independent person, and wondered what it would be like to 'defect' and go to live there. In 1961, while the company was performing in Paris, he got his chance. As Russian KGB (secret police) agents tried to force the rebellious dancer onto a plane back to Moscow, Nureyev threw himself on the mercy of the airport police — and was told he could stay in France.

Nureyev's defection made headlines around the world

The news of Rudolf Nureyev's defection made headlines in newspapers all over the world. Soon all sorts of stories were circulating in the dance world. People learned that Nureyev had started dancing against the wishes of his strict father, who considered dancing an unsuitable hobby for a boy; that he had gone to the Kirov ballet school at the very late age of 17, and that he went straight into the company dancing leading roles. Like everyone else, Margot Fonteyn was intrigued by the stories she heard. When she found herself called upon to arrange a gala performance in London, she decided to phone Rudolf Nureyev and ask him to appear in it.

Nureyev was so flattered to be invited by the famous ballerina that he accepted, even though he was flooded with work from all over Europe. His performance at the gala was a great success, and although he did not dance with Margot Fonteyn on this occasion, plans were soon afoot for him to become her partner in a Royal Ballet production of *Giselle*. At first, Margot Fonteyn objected, saying that she was too old to work with such a young dancer, but her husband Tito persuaded her to try, and she soon changed her mind. As rehearsals progressed, she realized that Rudolf Nureyev was not only an ideal Albrecht (Giselle's lover), he was also an ideal partner for her. He was imaginative, innovative and wild, while she was experienced, conservative and thoughtful. Despite the difference in their ages, personalities and backgrounds, the two dancers soon became firm friends, and remained so for the rest of their lives.

Tickets for *Giselle* went on sale, and the theatre box office was flooded with people wanting to attend. In all, 70,000 ballet fans tried to buy tickets for only three performances! On opening night, those lucky enough to have seats arrived at the Royal Opera House at Covent Garden. Many of the people in the audience were **balletomanes** who had seen *Giselle* before, but they had never seen a production of the ballet like this one. From the moment Rudolf Nureyev appeared on stage, he *was* Albrecht, the prince who tricks Giselle into believing he will marry her. And Margot Fonteyn — in her forties, and 20 years older than the character she was dancing — *was* Giselle. When she and Nureyev danced together, Fonteyn wrote later, she believed completely in the story they were acting out.

The first night of *Giselle* ended with an incredible 30 curtain calls. Everyone who saw it was convinced they had been present at a great moment in dance history. But what was the secret of the unlikely partnership's success?

The sort of partnership Fonteyn and Nureyev had was

very different to the ones ballet-goers had been used to. Although there had been famous male dancers, like Australian Robert Helpmann, for the last century the superstars of ballet had all been women. Rudolf Nureyev demanded that he be given equal attention, even reworking old ballets to give himself a larger part when necessary (he had a habit of making up his own steps, which audiences loved, though it often made him unpopular with other dancers). For the first time in many years, ballet-goers were seeing an equal partnership, where the male dancer was just as important as the woman. Nureyev's dancing was passionate, unpredictable and exciting, and when he found himself paired with a dancer as experienced and brilliant as Margot Fonteyn — herself perhaps the most famous ballerina in the world — audiences found the results electrifying.

Triumph followed triumph. Ballet fans queued for days to buy tickets to their performances, and they were in demand all over the world. When they performed *Swan Lake* together in Vienna, the audience gave them a record 89 curtain calls! Nor were they only successful in old favorites like *Giselle*. Ballets were choreographed especially for them, the most famous of which was *Marguerite and Armand*. People in the audience were moved to tears by the sad tale of the dying Marguerite and her young lover, and when the curtain fell at the end of the first performance there was total silence in the theater for several seconds. The audience was just too overcome to clap. Indeed, Fonteyn and Nureyev made such an

Ballet fans queued for days

impression in these roles that the ballet has never been danced by anybody else. Their performances have become a legend that no other dancers could possibly live up to.

The Fonteyn-Nureyev partnership was always successful, but not always a smooth one. Other dancers were jealous of the famous pair, particularly principals in the Royal Ballet who suddenly found themselves missing out on all the best parts. And although Margot Fonteyn was respected everywhere as a charming and gracious woman, people who knew and worked with Rudolf Nureyev described him as a very difficult man. When people annoyed him he would turn and attack them, screaming and swearing, sometimes even throwing things at them. (In one incident that was reported in papers all over the world, he hurled a glass of wine at a waiter who had asked him to help himself to some food. 'Nureyev doesn't wait on himself!' the great dancer screamed.)

Sometimes Nureyev even turned on Margot Fonteyn. When he didn't like her dancing, he would swear at her and throw temper tantrums which horrified people who saw them. Luckily, Margot Fonteyn knew just how to handle her fiery partner. When Rudolf lost his temper, she would let him rant and rave, then say something funny to make him laugh. She called him her 'little Genghis Khan', and said dancing with him was like dancing with a tiger. However, Margot Fonteyn also had her share of problems. Her husband Tito, a diplomat from Panama in Central America, was shot in an assassination attempt in 1964. His injuries left him a quadriplegic, unable to move

Like dancing with a tiger

or even to talk for the rest of his life.

After spending several years as partners, thrilling the world with their performances, Margot Fonteyn and Rudolf Nureyev began to dance less and less together. Margot Fonteyn was growing older, and looking towards the time when she would retire, while Rudolf Nureyev was eager to take on new projects, dancing with other partners, choreographing and directing ballets. The couple danced together for the last time in 1977, 15 years after their first appearance, when Margot Fonteyn was an amazing 58 years old. But for the people who saw them together in their greatest moments, the memory of classical ballet's 'perfect partnership' will never fade.

Did you know?

All ballet students are familiar with the five positions of the arms and feet. But there is more to classical ballet than that. According to some experts, when you take into account the various combinations, the full number of ballet positions is an incredible 39,850!

The leotards worn by many dancers to practice and perform in were originally made for flying, not dancing! They were invented in the nineteenth century by the French trapeze artist, Jules Leotard.

Dancing Life

Fancy Footwear: the Story of the Ballet Shoe

●●●●●●

Few people depend more on their feet than a ballet dancer — and few people rely more on their shoes. Like an athlete's running shoe, a dancer's leather or satin slipper is a highly specialized piece of equipment. A good ballet shoe can support the foot, make dancing safe and comfortable, and help its wearer turn in a great performance. To dance successfully and safely, a dancer needs all the help she can get from her shoes.

All beginning ballet students choosing their first pair of shoes are urged by their teachers to buy the best quality and fit they can find. An old, badly fitting or poorly made shoe can lead to serious injury for its wearer. Making do with second-best is simply not worth the risk. For a female ballet dancer, finding a well-made pointe or toe shoe — which enables her to dance on her toes — is even more important. Dancing on pointe looks graceful on stage, but it is actually a very unnatural way for human beings to move (as well as dangerous without proper training).

Luckily for modern dancers, there is a huge range of pointe shoes available, and most people can find a brand that suits them. However, 150 years ago, when ballerinas like Marie Taglioni began dancing on pointe for the first time, dancers had to make do with what they could get. Their soft shoes must have been terribly uncomfortable, and although they sometimes padded out the toes, the shoes must also have been dangerous to dance in. Later, shoemakers realized that a specialized sort of slipper was needed for this difficult type of dancing. Gradually the design of the ballet shoe was adapted to dancers' needs.

Today, a pointe shoe has a hard, square toe part (the block) made out of canvas and glue, which gives support to the dancer's foot and helps her keep her balance. The front part of the shoe (the vamp) is sewn onto two back parts, and attached to a leather sole, and there is a drawstring to help keep the shoe on. Making a good ballet shoe is an art, and in the past, they were all completely made by hand (in Russia they still are). Good makers were keenly sought after. Anna Pavlova, the famous Russian ballerina, would send all the way to Milan

Good makers were keenly sought after

in Italy for shoes. They were made especially for her and she ordered them 12 dozen (144) at a time! In her opinion, shoes made in factories 'had no soul', and she usually refused to dance in them.

Nowadays most ballet shoes are made in factories. Cutting machines stamp the pieces out exactly so that a worker can sew them together. However, the shoes are still finished by hand, and doing the elaborate pleating where the upper meets the sole is a highly skilled job. Modern manufacturers like Australian Paul Wright (himself a former dancer) are very aware of a dancer's needs, and go out of their way to provide shoes that are comfortable, attractive and safe for dancers to wear.

When you buy a new pair of ballet shoes, there is no difference between the right and left foot. It is the dancer who has to decide which shoe is best on which foot, and 'wear in' the shoes until they are comfortable. Everybody knows how stiff and uncomfortable new shoes can sometimes be, but for a professional dancer tight or loosely fitting shoes can be agony. (Imagine dancing on pointe on blistered toes: ouch!) Many dancers do terrible things to their new pointe shoes to try and break them in quickly, like throwing them at walls, hitting them with bricks, slashing the sole with a Stanley knife, and tearing the insole out completely. The shoes come without ribbons or elastics, so the dancer also has to sew these on, and dull the shiny satin with calamine lotion before they are ready to wear. Not surprisingly, pointe shoes rarely last long. Some dancers are heavier on shoes than others, and can wear a pair out in a single performance; few pointe shoes last more than a week with heavy usage. For this reason, a dancer will always have several pairs of shoes 'on the go' at any time, all in different stages of wear.

> *A dancer will have several pairs of shoes 'on the go' at any time*

Many professional dancers have their shoes personally fitted to the exact shape of their foot. Others try all sorts and makes until they find one they like and then stick with it. Mysteriously, though, shoes of the same size and make can sometimes feel amazingly different to the individual dancer. 'Some,' wrote Margot Fonteyn, 'are a dream to wear, and others are just wrong from the start. They are the bane of every ballerina's life.'

How to Look After your Ballet Shoes

Here are some hints for getting your new shoes ready to wear, and advice for keeping them in good shape.
- Always buy good-quality, satin ribbon (not nylon hair ribbon). The best place to buy this is at a specialist dance shop,which will stock good brands, and be able to help you find the right width and color.

Make sure you buy the correct flesh-colored ribbon to match the shoe, not pink.

- Don't skimp on ribbon! Adult dancers recommend about 6 ½ feet for a pair. There should be enough ribbon to cross over your foot at the front, and wrap twice around your ankle to tie in a neat knot (not a bow) at the back outside ankle. (This is the part which doesn't show when your feet are turned out.) Remember, it is always easier to trim long ribbons than lengthen ones which are too short.

- Find the right place to sew the ribbons by bending in the heel of the shoe to lie flat against the sides. The ribbon should be sewn on by hand at this spot. If you have trouble, try using a thimble to push the needle through. Another dancer's tip is to use fine crochet thread to sew your ribbons on. Ordinary sewing thread can rot and snap after being rubbed by your sweaty foot; the crochet thread is stronger.

- Always fold the end of the ribbon over at least ½-¾" before you begin to sew. Folding the ribbon keeps it from fraying inside your shoe, and perhaps breaking or pulling loose while you are dancing. You should also trim the loose ends of the ribbon diagonally — this stops it unraveling and looking ugly.

- Some professional dancers suggest that you sew dressmaker's tape on the inside to make the ribbons especially strong. This helps them use their ribbons over and over again. If you buy good-quality ribbon, and take care of your shoes, you should be able to recycle the ribbon onto the next pair.

- Take care of your shoes by wearing them only in class. Ballet shoes are very soft, and nothing wears them out more quickly than walking on hard, everyday surfaces like concrete.

- When you've arrived home from class, make sure you hang your sweaty shoes up to dry, so they'll be ready for next time. This is particularly important with pointe shoes, which can easily become soft and dangerous to dance in.

Injury

● ● ● ● ● ●

If there is one thing all dancers dread, it is injuring themselves. For an ordinary person, strained muscles, ligament problems and stress fractures are bad enough: in a dancer, they spell disaster. Injuries mean working and performing in constant pain, or they mean time off from dancing, perhaps the loss of the technique and fitness the dancer has worked so hard to build up. At worst, a truly serious injury can finish a dancer's career for good.

Nowadays, all dancers are trained to understand the way their bodies work. Dance teachers, physiotherapists and doctors who specialize in treating dancers emphasize the importance of preventing injuries instead of curing them. But in real life, it is not always possible to prevent accidents. Sadly, almost every serious dancer will suffer injury at some point in their career.

Dancers are most likely to be injured when they are tired and overworked. Despite their training, which is designed to build up strength and flexibility, some young dancers will push themselves too far. And experienced dancers can succumb to stress injuries which build up over a long time, or make silly mistakes when they are tired or run down. Another time dancers are particularly at risk of injury is when they come back to work after going away on vacation, being ill, or taking some other sort of break. On their return they try and pick up exactly where they left off, forgetting that their bodies need to work their way back gradually into condition.

A dancer's greatest protection against injury is a strong body, good training, and safe conditions to dance in. Dancing on a concrete floor (which is hard to fall on, and jars the bones and muscles of working dancers) is a recipe for disaster. So are old or worn-out dance shoes.

Not surprisingly, different types of dancers are prone to different types of injuries. Female ballet dancers, for example, are most often injured in the legs. This is because their knees, ankles and feet are the parts of their bodies most under stress when dancing. Male ballet dancers run the risk of back and neck injuries because of the heavy lifting they have to do.

Belly dancers move in completely different ways to other dancers, and are prone to injuries of the lower back and knees. Yani, a professional belly dancer and teacher, says most of the belly dancing injuries she has seen are due to dancers having a poor technique, or not warming up properly before they go out to perform. 'This advice goes for any sort of dancing,' says Yani, firmly. 'If you do things properly, you should

'If you do things properly, you should be able to avoid most injuries'

be able to avoid most injuries.'

However, Yani herself has been plagued by problems with her little toe, which has a tendency to dislocate if it is knocked or bumped. Doctors and physiotherapists can do nothing to help when this happens, so Yani has to cope by packing her foot with ice and strapping the toe so tightly it can't move. Going out to dance barefoot like this is always a problem, but luckily belly dancing does not have to involve a lot of complicated footwork, so she can put pressure on other parts of her foot, or favor that foot and rely mostly on the uninjured one.

Another dancer who has had to cope with a devastating injury — and worse — is Nicola Oliver. In 1986, Nicola was 17, and a dedicated dance student. She was practicing hard for an important exam, and working on her dancing six hours a day. At the same time she was performing with a semi-professional dance company in a production of the ballet *Beauty and the Beast*. One day, while dancing in the ballet, Nicola dislocated her knee.

'Of course, I knew immediately something was wrong,' she says, 'but I didn't realize it was anything serious. I just bought a knee guard and put it on. The next day I could hardly walk.'

It later turned out that Nicola had been born with a knee problem nobody knew about. Under the strain of all the work she was doing, her knee was literally giving up. At the time though, all that mattered to Nicola was the ballet she was supposed to be dancing in. At the next performance, she turned up as usual at the theater. As soon as she took off her knee guard to start warming up, she collapsed backstage.

'I did one pirouette and just crumpled up,' Nicola says. 'I had to try and teach somebody else my steps, and then I borrowed ten dollars and went straight to the hospital in a taxi. I missed the performance completely.'

Nicola's dance injury was a serious one. She had not only dislocated her knee, she had torn an important ligament in it. There was no question now of her dancing in the ballet, or doing the exam she had worked so hard for. Instead, she spent hours and hours with a physiotherapist, desperately trying to heal her injury. But her knee kept dislocating, and eventually she had to have an operation on it. After she had recovered from this, Nicola went back to dancing. Within a year, her other knee collapsed too, and Nicola's worst fears were realized. Her dancing career was over.

Today Nicola is philosophical about what happened, but she admits that at the time it was very hard. 'When you're

> **'You're left with a terrible emptiness in your life'**

doing something all day, six days a week, and then suddenly it's not there, you're left with a terrible emptiness in your life. At first, when I couldn't dance, I spent all my time watching other people. But gradually other things have come into my life, and my great love of dance is still there.'

Happily, Nicola was able to make a career in dance after all. She went on to become a dance teacher and choreographer, work she finds exciting and fulfilling. 'I love trying to pass on the joy dancing gives me to the kids,' she says. 'After all, joy is what dancing's all about.'

First Aid for Dancers

If you have an accident in your dance class, your teacher should be able to help you until you can see a physiotherapist or doctor. However, dance students practicing at home are also at risk. If you do have an accident, here is some basic first aid which physiotherapists recommend for minor strains and sprains.

First, it is important to rest the injured body part. Apply an ice pack from the freezer. (It is a good idea to buy one from a pharmacist if you are doing a lot of serious practice, but a packet of frozen peas wrapped in a towel will do in an emergency.) Then wrap the injured part in a firm ace bandage and keep it elevated on pillows or in a suitable sling.

If you follow these instructions carefully, you should keep any swelling to a minimum. After 24 hours, when healing has begun, it is important to begin gentle movement. This encourages the injured part to stay flexible, not heal up tight and stiff to give you problems in the future.

And of course, don't just rely on these instructions. All dance injuries should be thoroughly checked out by an expert. Make sure you go and see a physiotherapist, who can teach you the correct exercises, and help with other treatments such as ultrasound to get you back on the road to recovery.

Dancing Footballers

Most people realize that a dancer's training is physically and mentally very stressful — and few know this better than some footballers in England and the United States! In the 1970s, these footballers were asked to attend a series of ballet classes, and compare the dancers' training with their own. The footballers — not trained in ballet, but

physically extremely fit — were amazed at how difficult and
exhausting the work was. At the end of the course, they agreed that the
average dancer worked much harder than they did, and were glad to
get back on the playing field!

A Dancing World

Magical Dance

● ● ● ● ● ●

For as long as there have been people on Earth, there has been dancing. Somehow, it has always seemed natural for human beings to move their bodies in time to rhythms and music — even when these are heard only in their own heads. Today we usually think of dancing as a fun pastime, or a performance which takes place on a stage. But early people took dancing much more seriously. For them, dancing was something powerful and magical.

Early people believed the right dance could please the gods, make the crops grow and the rain fall, or give success in battle. Good hunting might be ensured by a dance which showed an animal or bird being hunted down and killed. Dances like this are still performed today by many Australian Aboriginal peoples.

Dances were also a way of celebrating when something good happened in a community. A group of people would join hands and dance joyfully in a circle — just as today, guests at weddings will stand in a ring to see off the bride and groom. Other times for dancing included the big turning points in individual people's lives — when they were born, when they became adults, and when they died; times of religious ceremony. Sometimes, the dances were simply an act of praise or worship. When Moses' sister Miriam danced before God in the Bible story, she was using dance to show her joy, and to say thank you for the Jewish people's escape from slavery in Egypt.

Religious and magical dances like these sometimes had to be performed by a special person or groups of people within the community. Warriors would dance a war dance, for example, and hunters would dance the hunting dance. Other dances had to be performed at a particular time of year, or even in a special place. Nowadays, dancing around the maypole on 1 May is done mostly for fun, and many schools will have a maypole at fairs. But it was originally a fertility dance, meant to make the crops grow and the farm animals increase. It was performed at the beginning of the European summer, because that was the most fertile time of the year. Many other folk dances which are danced on special days were also originally religious dances (English Morris dances are a good example). Later, when people's religious beliefs changed, they forgot what the dances meant, but kept on dancing them out of habit, and because they liked doing them.

For the dances to work properly, it was often necessary to keep them secret. They would be taught only to men or women who had been through an initiation ceremony: a special ritual which made a person ready to know certain secrets, or take on a particular role in the community. (The most common initiation ceremonies are those performed when a young person grows up.) Another way of keeping the sacred dance secret was to perform it in a secret location. Many of the secret-sacred sites modern Aboriginal people try so hard to hold onto are places where such dancing takes place. Aboriginal people also use their dances to teach their sacred stories and history. Because their culture is an oral one (one in which things are not written down), dance is an important way of handing down information to the next generation.

Today, dancing is still used in worship by people of many religious faiths, particularly in Eastern religions like Hinduism, Shinto and Confucianism. Many people have seen Hare Krishna followers singing and dancing in the city, but how many have stopped to think about what they are actually doing? They are not just dancing around for no reason, they are dancing to worship God. 'When we dance, it's not like a formal thing where you learn steps,' explains Tirtharaj dasa, an Australian Hare Krishna devotee. 'It's spontaneous. We dance out of ecstasy and praise.' Hare Krishna people usually sing or chant while they dance. This chanting is called a *kirtan*, which means 'worship of God'.

Hare Krishna dancing is very ancient. The dancers do not do it to show off, or draw attention to themselves, but as something beautiful and joyous. 'If somebody feels happy, they jump for joy,' Tirtharaj dasa says.

Another person who believes dancing is all about showing joy is Nicola Oliver. Nicola is a member of St. Bartholomew's, a large suburban Episcopalian church. She is also a professional dance teacher and choreographer. At St. Bartholomew's, Nicola is in charge of a team of dancers, all members of the congregation, who perform at church services and on special occasions. 'The Bible says to praise God "with timbrel and dance",' Nicola explains, 'and that is what we are trying to do. When we dance, we are not performing so much as worshipping God with movement. We pray and think very hard about what we are doing. It's what you feel in your heart that's important.'

Church dance groups are becoming very common in all denominations. Nicola herself runs four different groups, including one for teenagers which is very energetic and modern in style, and one for children which teaches them basic dance. She also runs a timbrel (tamborine) group. This is a special type of religious dancing in which all of the timbrel movements have individual meanings. The movements form patterns that tell a story or message, and these are combined with steps to form a dance. 'People tend to think of timbrel as being loud and jangly, like the Salvation Army,' says Nicola, 'but it can also be quite soft. In one dance I've just choreographed, you can hardly hear the tamborine at all. Done well, it can be very beautiful.'

The Fairies' Dancing Ring

In many fairy books, a fairy ring is drawn as a circle of red and white-spotted toadstools. But real fairy rings, the lush green circles which can sometimes be seen in fields, are actually places for fairies to dance.

The fairies live in a village underneath the ring and come up at night to do their wild dances in the open air. Brave or curious people who run from right to left around a fairy ring at the full moon will hear the sound of their laughter deep in the ground. Never go near a fairy ring at Halloween, though – on that night, anyone who ventures into one falls into the fairies' power, and you might find yourself dancing with them forever...

Strictly Belly Dancing

It's 9 P.M. and there's a line of people outside an inner-city nightclub, waiting to go in. It's a sight which can be seen in big cities all over Australia — but the people who are patiently queuing to get into this particular nightclub are not waiting to see a popular rock group or singer. They've come to see one thing only, and the sign outside on the sidewalk gives a clue to what it is. *Yani...Rasheeda's Veils...* Tonight's entertainment is strictly belly dancing!

Inside, a feast of belly dancing is just beginning. Laurel Victoria Gray, an American, has just spent two dangerous and exciting years in Uzbekistan (near Afghanistan), teaching and learning the local dances. Cousins Jacinda and Morgiana (from Sydney) are about to take their own version of belly dance to Japan; they enjoy mixing belly dance with other types of dancing, and sometimes dance to rock music. Rasheeda's Veils perform not only traditional Egyptian cane dances (based on men's martial arts movements), but dances they have choreographed themselves to film soundtracks, country and western songs, and Western classical music. By the end of the evening, one thing is certain. Belly dancing is not only incredibly popular — it is an amazingly versatile type of dance.

Nobody knows exactly when or where belly dancing started. However, we do know that it is very ancient, because there are pictures of belly dancers on the walls of Egyptian tombs, dating back almost 3,500 years. Today, belly dancing is done by people in Turkey, Egypt, Greece, northern Africa, the Middle East, and even parts of India and Pakistan.

In the late nineteenth and early twentieth centuries, people in the West began to take an interest in Middle Eastern culture. Explorers like Sir Richard Burton and Isabelle Eberhardt wrote accounts of their journeys there, and romances with titles like *The Lure of the Desert* became very popular. These were followed in the 1920's by films like *The Sheikh*, starring the handsome actor-dancer Rudolph Valentino. Neither the romances nor the films were very accurate. Even today, most Western people think of belly dancers as beautiful women with brief, spangly costumes and jewels in their belly button, who dance in nightclubs and let men tuck money under their bra straps.

This picture is quite wrong. In fact, belly dancing was originally done by women for other women. Even less well known is the fact that there is also a tradition of belly dancing for men! (Today, the world's highest paid belly dancers are actually male.) In the Middle Eastern countries where belly dancing originated, men and women led almost separate lives. Women were very strictly guarded by their male relatives, and the wives and daughters of wealthy men were literally shut away from the outside world in special women's quarters called harems. Life in the harem was slow-paced and boring, so the women would often while away the hours by dancing for each other, sometimes just for fun, sometimes to

> Today, the world's highest paid belly dancers are actually male

celebrate some special event. When a woman had a baby, for example, her companions would dance for her while she was in labor. They believed their dancing would encourage the baby to be born. Belly dancing was also done by pregnant women, because the movements helped strengthen the stomach muscles used in giving birth.

The clothes worn by these women while they were dancing were not at all like the spangly costumes we are used to. In fact, they were very modest. A typical outfit would consist of a jacket or bolero-type vest, over a long dress or shift, which would in turn be worn over a pair of trousers. There was no flesh showing at all, far less anybody's belly! In other cultures (for example among the Romany or gipsy people) the women would wear long skirts, but draw attention to their hips by tying a brightly colored scarf around them. Ordinary wives and mothers would have been shocked at the thought of dancing in front of men at all, far less dancing in the sexy, revealing clothes we are used to. (Even today in Saudi Arabia, women will not let themselves be photographed dancing — just in case a man sees the picture.) As a result, the belly dancers seen by visitors from the West were not-very-respectable women who were dancing — and dressing — purely to impress men. This idea of belly dancing as a tacky display of veils and sequins passed into popular books and films. Even the jewel in the belly button is a Western idea. When belly dancers began appearing in Hollywood movies, film directors thought it was immodest for a woman to show her navel on screen, and solved the problem by covering it with a spangle!

Today, belly dancing differs greatly from place to place, culture to culture. Some forms of belly dancing concentrate on moving the hips, while others emphasize the top part of the body. Men's belly dancing usually concentrates on wriggling the shoulders and chest, while in Uzbekistan, where Laurel Victoria Gray studied, most of the movement is in the hands, shoulders and feet. She says this is partly due to influence from India, partly due to the women's clothes. Her own beautiful red and gold costume, which she bought when she was staying there, literally covers her from head to foot — there's not much point moving parts of the body which can't be seen!

Little girls in Uzbekistan learn to dance not by having lessons, but by watching older women. By copying their mothers, they automatically grow up dancing in the same style, and in this way the dances are passed down from one generation to the next. Some, though not all, belly-dancing teachers will teach children, but it is a difficult and demanding style of dancing to learn. Megan Banach, who runs the Isis Bellydance School, says that to belly dance successfully you need to be fit, flexible, and strong. Megan's lessons begin with about 10 minutes of stretching exercises, followed by strengthening exercises. After this, her students spend time doing a basic drill of pelvic movements. 'These exercises are really boring,' says Megan, 'but it's good to have discipline in the basic movements before you try to put in your own interpretation.' As with many types of dancing, it is also important to have the right body type. Although thin women can and do belly dance successfully, belly dancers need to be very fluid, and large women always look more beautiful and graceful. Some belly dancers have such amazing muscle control that they can flip coins with their stomach muscles!

Some belly dancers can flip coins with their stomach muscles!

As well as the traditional dances which are handed down from generation to generation, modern dancers are also free to make up their own choreography. Many people like to work the steps out completely in advance; others, like Brisbane dancer Yani, prefer to improvize. Yani says that until she goes out to perform, she never knows exactly how she is going to dance. This sounds very difficult, but Yani says that the secret is to know the music very thoroughly beforehand. A lot of belly-dancing music sounds strange to Western people, but while the rhythms are different to the ones we're used to, many of the instruments are the same as or similar to ones we know. Clarinets, flutes and violins are all used, as well as more exotic instruments like the Greek *bazouki* and a special hand drum called the *darbuka*. Yani also uses instruments herself to help her dancing : bells around her ankles, and special finger cymbals called *zils*. By knowing the rhythms perfectly in advance, she says she is able to interpret the music to its best advantage, but she also says that you can belly dance to practically any music you like. 'Belly dancing is an expression of joy and womanliness,' she says. 'In the end, it's your own personal interpretation that counts.'

The Dance of the Hairy Spider

The tarantula is a huge hairy spider from southern Italy. In the past, it was believed that the tarantula's bite caused a mysterious disease called 'tarantism' — a disease which had only one cure. The victim, doctors maintained, had to dance a wild, rapid dance called a *tarantella* until the disease was driven from the body. In areas where the tarantula was common, traveling fiddlers would move about the fields during the harvest, just in case one of the workers was bitten.

Other people said that the bite of the spider actually *caused* the urge to dance. In this case, the unlucky victim would dance the tarantella until he or she dropped dead from exhaustion.

Modern doctors tell us that the bite of the tarantula isn't especially harmful, and that the people who claimed to have been cured by dancing the tarantella would probably have recovered anyway. But the legend of the dance of the hairy spider lives on. Many famous composers have written 'tarantella' music, and people dance tarantellas to this very day.

Cook's Hornpipe

The hornpipe is a lively dance traditionally performed by sailors on board ship. The explorer, Captain James Cook, was a great believer in hornpipes. On his journeys to Antarctica, the east coast of Australia and Hawaii, Captain Cook made his sailors dance them as often as possible. He believed the dancing was an important way of keeping the men healthy and happy.

The Dancing Universe

Nowadays we know that the Earth and all the other planets revolve around the Sun. But in the Middle Ages, astronomers had not yet worked out exactly how the solar system moved. Medieval people believed that the Earth was surrounded by a series of spheres — a bit like a Russian doll.

Each sphere held the moon, the sun, or the stars, or one of the planets. The whole nest of spheres rotated around the Earth, and as they moved, they made a beautiful noise. This strange, unearthly sound was known as the 'Music of the Spheres'. Because of this belief, and because of the stately way the stars and planets moved across the sky, medieval people liked to think that they were dancing.

The very last sphere was right next to heaven, where God lived. It was known in Latin as the *Primum Mobile* or 'first mover', because it made all the other spheres go around. The Primum Mobile could not be seen from Earth, which meant that artists trying to draw pictures of the universe had to use their imagination. They solved the problem by drawing the Primum Mobile as a young girl, dancing slowly in a wide graceful circle and tossing her sphere as she danced like a golden ball.

Kings and Congas

● ● ● ● ● ●

Over the centuries different types of dancing have come in and out of fashion — just like the clothes we wear, or the furniture we use in our houses. And just as today few people would be likely to go out wearing pointy shoes with toes over a foot long, or the tall cone-like hats medieval women wore, so most modern people prefer dancing modern dances.

Today we don't know a great deal about the way people danced in the Middle Ages. Experts who specialize in these dances are almost like archaeologists, reconstructing the steps from paintings and old manuscripts, some of them written in languages which are no longer even spoken. They also have to understand how medieval life was different to our own. For example, while it now seems quite normal for dancers to dance alone, or in pairs, boy with girl, this was not always the case. The earliest dances from the Western world were line or circle dances, in which groups of people linked hands or arms and danced in a procession, or around in a ring. One medieval dance which has survived, the *farandole*, is a bit like an early version of a conga line, and usually ends with the dancers being tied up in knots!

> *The earliest dances from the Western world were line or circle dances*

The idea of men and women dancing together in couples dates from about the twelfth century. This was the

age of troubadors and love songs, when a knight would choose a lady to admire, and send her love poetry before going out to fight in a tournament. As the lady was usually somebody else's wife or daughter, her admirer would not get very many opportunities to be with her. Dancing together in public meant that the couple could enjoy each other's company, and even hold hands, while remaining completely respectable. By the 1400s, a period in history known as the Renaissance, dancing in couples was normal in courts and grand houses all over Europe.

Today, Renaissance dance is becoming popular again. People interested in the music and history of the time spend years researching dances, music and costumes. They find detective work like this fun and rewarding, and their interest in dance often leads to all sorts of new skills, like making costumes and early musical instruments.

Dressing up in costume is popular with Renaissance dance groups, because it makes their performances look colorful and interesting. However, it also helps us understand why people in those days danced the way they did. In the sixteenth century, for example, European women wore hoops called farthingales under their skirts, and tightly-laced wooden corsets around their bodies. Men padded their clothes with horsehair or even sawdust. Both men and women wore several layers of clothing to keep warm, and would often be seen wearing cartwheel-like collars or ruffs so big they could scarcely turn their heads. Stiff, uncomfortable clothes like these meant that the dancing had to be dignified and stately. Slow processional dances like the *pavan* were often used to open banquets and other grand social occasions, because they gave the ladies and gentlemen of the court the opportunity to parade around and show off their latest finery.

Other dances like the *galliard* and *la volta* could be very energetic, but good manners were always of utmost importance. Renaissance books about dancing devote pages and pages to explaining how dancers should speak and hold themselves, and how they should bow or curtsey. In one book, dancers are even told to 'spit and blow your nose sparingly', and are advised to use a handkerchief if they have to! Nevertheless, despite having to be careful how they behaved themselves, Renaissance people loved to dance as much as we do. A well-known picture shows the great English Queen, Elizabeth I, dancing *la volta* with her admirer, the Earl of Leicester.

Another famous monarch was one of the most influential dancers of the next century. King Louis XIV of France, who lived from 1648 to 1715, was a passionate and talented dancer. Huge *ballets de cour* (court ballets) were staged at his palace at Versailles every year, and although these grand productions were nothing like our modern 'ballets', this is where the name comes from. The King spared no expense on sets, costumes, music or special effects, and he expected all his nobles to take part in them. By today's standards, these ballets were very, very long. *Le Ballet de la Nuit* — in which the 14-year-old Louis appeared as the Rising Sun — lasted an incredible 13 hours!

Le Ballet de la Nuit *lasted an incredible 13 hours!*

All noble children, boys and girls, studied dancing seriously from a very young age. Although the dancing they learned was very different to that which is taught in modern dance schools, some things — for example, the dancer's turned-out legs, and the five positions of the feet — would be familiar to modern ballet students. (Even today all ballet terms are French.) There was, however, no undignified leaping about. In King Louis' ballets, the dancers moved through a series of stately poses, to music written especially by some of France's best composers. Everything was graceful and elegant, from the steps to the storylines. French seventeenth-century ballets were full of gods, spirits, and even magic, which created plenty of opportunity for exciting and spectacular special effects. One ballet 'festival' held in 1664 lasted three days, and finished with a battle between three sea monsters, the appearance of an 'enchanted palace' and an exploding island — all made of fireworks!

A Daring Dancer. . .

Today, although there are many talented male dancers, most people tend to think of professional dancers as being women. In the past, this was far from the case — perhaps because appearing on the stage was not considered respectable. In France the first time professional women dancers performed was in 1681. Fifty years later another French woman dancer caused an even bigger scandal. Sick of the way her male partners were given all the applause for their fancy footwork, Marie-Anne Cupis de Camargo shocked audiences by shortening her skirts to reveal her steps — and her ankle!

...and A Keen Conductor

King Louis XIV's ballets were accompanied by music written by some of the finest composers in France. One of these composers, Jean-Baptiste Lully, died very strangely. While beating time vigorously with a conducting stick — a staff almost as tall as he was — he got so excited he banged it right through his foot, and died shortly afterwards of blood poisoning.

The Morris Marathon

Morris dancing is a form of folk dancing from England. It is very energetic, and is usually danced by groups of men who wear bells on their clothes, and clash heavy sticks together as part of the dance.

One of the most famous Morris dancers of all was Will Kempe, a comic actor who worked with the playwright William Shakespeare in the late sixteenth century. In 1600 Kemp became an instant celebrity when, for a bet, he danced a Morris from London to Norwich — an amazing 114 miles away! The dance took nine days over what would have been terrible roads. When he had finished Kempe wrote and published an account of it called *Kemps morris to Norwiche*.

Anna Pavlova's Legacy: The Birth of the Australian Ballet

● ● ● ● ● ●

Touring is part of a dancer's life — and no dancer in history toured quite so enthusiastically as the great Anna Pavlova. Even though there was no air travel to speak of in her day, and all journeys had to be made by train or ship, Anna and her company of dancers traveled to almost every continent on Earth. Anna Pavlova's mission was to take dance to the whole world. Nobody who saw her dance ever forgot the experience, and one of the countries on which her visit left a lasting impression was Australia.

Anna Pavlova visited Australia twice, in 1926 and 1929. In those days, there was no Australian Ballet, or any other professional Australian dance company, so when the great Pavlova announced she was going to visit, there was tremendous excitement. Nowadays, it would be almost unthinkable for an international dance company to visit small country towns, but Anna and her dancers began their 1929 tour in Townsville in north Queensland, and gradually worked their way down the eastern coast, eventually finishing in Perth. Tickets sold out in theater after theater, the tour was a triumph, and a Western Australian chef was even inspired to invent a dessert – the 'pavlova'.

Anna Pavlova liked Australia very much. However, she thought it very sad that all the promising Australian

dancers had to go overseas to train and work. During her
visits, Anna Pavlova did everything she
could to meet young dancers, and
encourage the ones she thought were
talented.

> *All the
> promising
> Australian
> dancers
> had to go
> overseas*

One of the dancers she met was a
South Australian boy called Robert
Helpmann. Ever since he was tiny,
Robert had wanted to go on stage, and
after attending classes with Pavlova's
company, he decided to devote his life to
dancing. But in the 1920s and 1930s, there were no real
opportunities in Australia, so Robert Helpmann had to
leave and go to London. Here he joined the Royal Ballet,
danced with ballerinas like Margot Fonteyn, and
choreographed many successful ballets of his own.
He became Australia's first internationally famous ballet
dancer, and a celebrated actor and director. But although
he returned to Australia to work later in life, he still had to
move away to get his career established.

Luckily, in Australia, this situation was about to change
— and in a roundabout way, this was due to Anna Pavlova!
When Anna's company toured in 1929, one of the popular
ballets it performed was *Giselle*, and in this particular
production the role of Giselle's jilted admirer Hilarion was
taken by a Czech dancer called Edouard Borovansky.
Nearly 10 years later, in 1939, Borovansky visited Australia
again with another company. World War II had just broken
out in Europe, so the fiery Czech dancer decided to stay.
Full of exciting ideas, Borovansky and his wife Xenia began
by setting up a dance school in Melbourne. Then, in 1940

Borovansky established the Borovansky Australian Ballet. At last, Australia had a ballet company of its own.

Edouard Borovansky was a man of great energy and vision. His dancers loved and hated him at the same time, perhaps because he drove himself as relentlessly as he drove them. Throughout the 1940s and 1950s, his productions were constantly touring the country, providing work for many Australian dancers, and teaching a whole new generation of Australians to love ballet. But the pace this human dynamo set himself was too much. In 1959 Borovansky died of a heart attack at the early age of 57.

Without Borovansky to run it, his ballet company was left in disarray. However, because of his work, and because of people like Anna Pavlova who had bravely taken ballet halfway around the world, there was now a huge audience of ballet fans in Australia. People were used to being able to see ballet regularly, and what was more, they *wanted* to see it. Politicians, dancers, and the general public agreed. The time had come to set up a national ballet company for all Australians to enjoy.

> *There was now a huge audience of ballet fans in Australia*

Under the leadership of Peggy van Praagh, a talented Englishwoman, a brand-new ballet company was born out of what was left of the Borovansky company: the Australian Ballet. On 2 November 1962, the Australian Ballet gave its first performance of *Swan Lake*. Since then, it has become one of the world's great ballet companies.

Anna Pavlova would have been delighted.

The Way We Dance Now

● ● ● ● ● ●

Everybody loves to dance. However, the dances we do ourselves just for fun are often quite different to the dances we see professional dancers perform on stage. This sort of dancing is called social dancing, and one thing which is very obvious about it is the way different dances come quickly in and out of fashion.

The twentieth century has been full of new ways of dancing. One reason for this is improved communications and travel. Video clips show us the dances that go along with the latest hits, and we learn the steps we like by watching TV and copying them. We can even see famous musicians and dancers like Madonna in person — because modern jet travel allows her to tour and give concerts. Audio tapes and CDs make the latest dance songs available all around the world. Another reason is that nowadays people are more open to the idea of learning about other cultures and their dancing. A hundred and fifty years ago, people in America would have been very dubious about learning dances from South America, but in the twentieth century we have 'borrowed' the tango, the rumba, the samba, the cha-cha-cha, the lambada and many other dances from Latin America.

Today, as soon as a new dance craze takes off in London, New York or Rio de Janeiro, people all over the world are dancing it too. Because the twentieth century has been very rich in new types of popular music (all the different types of jazz, blues and rock are twentieth-century inventions) people are constantly being challenged to invent new ways of dancing. Record companies are very conscious of the huge market that exists for dance music. As soon as people begin dancing a particular dance — let's say, an imaginary dance called the Smash — in nightclubs, at parties, or just in their own home, record companies make sure they record and release more singles with the 'Smash' sound. Other times, they will deliberately find or invent a toe-tapping dance to accompany a new song. In the late 1980s, people in America went crazy over a funny dance called 'the chicken dance'. The dance was easy to do, and soon people everywhere were squawking and flapping their arms like chickens. But without the dance, who would have bought the single? Another way dancing is used to sell records is through movies. In 1994, the soundtrack to the Australian film *The Adventures of Priscilla: Queen of the Desert* shot to the top of the charts. Many of the songs on the soundtrack were famous disco songs from the 1970s, which were used in the movie for funny dance sequences. People liked them so much in the movie that they went straight out, and bought the CD.

As famous for their superb dance skills as for their singing

Record companies are also careful to include good dancing in videos, because they know that if people like the dancing, they will take the time to watch the clip and listen to the song. Pop stars like Madonna and Michael Jackson are as famous for their superb dance skills as for their singing. In fact, Madonna herself originally wanted to be a dancer. As a teenager she even won a dance scholarship, and hoped for a career with a famous modern dance company. Today Madonna prepares as long and hard for her stage shows as any other professional dancer, touring the world with a choreographer and her own personal fitness trainer. By employing top dancers to perform with her, she has made people realize just how exciting good dancing makes a pop concert. In fact, many of her fans believe Madonna is a better dancer than she is a singer!

Although people of all ages can and do dance, it is always easiest for people who are fit and young. Because the twentieth century has seen the arrival of rock and pop music which appeals most to young people, many modern dances are invented by and for young people to dance. **Jiving**, for example, was invented in the 1950s to go with the new rock and roll music played by people like Bill Haley and Buddy Holly. It was followed by a dance craze called the **twist**, which started in America with a song of the same name. (The Beatles' song 'Twist and Shout' was one of many attempts to cash in on the craze for this type of dancing.)

Today, new dances are invented in nightclubs to go with particular songs or types of music, while other types of dancing come straight from the street. Break dancing and rap dancing both originated on the streets of New York. Gangs of teenagers would challenge each other to 'dance duels', training and practicing hard in order to prove they were the best and coolest on the block.

Like everything else in our modern world, the way we dance is changing at a remarkable rate. In fact, there are almost as many different ways of dancing as there are people on Earth. Perhaps the next dance craze will come from Japan, or Paris, or even India. One thing is for certain: nobody can possibly guess which way human beings will be dancing next.

Crazy Dancing

The twentieth century has probably had more dance **crazes** than any other. Some of the dances are still famous: everybody, for example, has heard of the 1920s **Charleston**, and the 1950s **twist**, which one person has described as 'moving your feet as if you were trying to stub out a cigarette, and your hips as if you were drying your back with a towel'! Other dances have disappeared so quickly almost nobody remembers them today. Here are some particularly strange dances which have come briefly in — and out — of fashion since the turn of the century.

- The **bunny hug** and

The **turkey trot** were popular early in the century. (They were part of a craze for 'animal dances' of which only the foxtrot is still danced.)

■ The **Apache** was another early twentieth-century dance which did not really take off in the dance hall — it was far too violent! Male Apache dancers would literally throw their partners around the stage, and then pretend to strangle or knife them! People found the Apache exciting to watch, but few dared to risk it for themselves.

■ The **hokey pokey** is now thought of as a children's dance or game — but in the 1930s, before World War II, it was a craze in dance halls across Australia.

■ The great World War II dance craze was the **jitterbug**.

■ In the early 1960s, you might have found yourself dancing the

mashed potato (in which dancers stamped their feet as if they were squashing potatoes on the ground).

■ Later 1960s dances included **the penguin bounce**, the **robot** and the **dog**!

■ Another popular dance was the **bus stop**, while in the 1970s, people went to discos to dance **le freak**, and banged their hips together in a strange dance called the **bump**.

Since the early 1980s people have spun on their heads doing **break dancing**, **moonwalked** with Michael Jackson, kicked up their heels doing **flash dancing**, annoyed their parents with **dirty dancing**, flapped their arms dancing the **chicken dance**, and tied themselves in knots doing the **lambada**!

GLOSSARY

balletomane: a ballet fan, somebody who has a 'thing' about ballet

choreographer: the person who maps out the steps and dances in a production, and teaches them to the dancers

dance critic: a journalist with a special knowledge of dance who writes reviews of performances for a newspaper or magazine

debut: a dancer's first-ever performance

dress rehearsal: the very last rehearsal, in which everything (sets, costumes and music) is exactly as it will be in the first performance

gala: a special performance, often for charity, in which many famous dancers perform short items

notation systems: ways of writing dances down on paper, so that there is a record for future performers. Many ballet companies use Benesh Notation, which is written on five lines like a piece of music

pas de deux: a dance for two people

repertoire: the list of different productions a dance company can perform

READING LIST

Books marked * are adult books, but you will still find them interesting.

The Young Dancer
by Darcey Bussell
(RD Press, Sydney, 1994)

Ballet Company
by Kate Castle
(Franklin Watts, London, 1984)

The Magic of Dance
by Margot Fonteyn
(Knopf, New York, 1979)
This is an older book, still available in libraries and second-hand bookshops. It has dozens of beautiful pictures, and is a very interesting read.

The Complete Guide for Australian Dancers
by Charles Lisner
(Rigby, Melbourne, 1988)
An invaluable book for Australians, this includes chapters on dance history, classes and teachers, what to wear, dance injuries, and professional training and work.

The Australian Ballet: Twenty-one Years
by Charles Lisner
(University of Queensland Press, Brisbane, 1983)
The story of the famous ballet company, with many photographs

Dance
by Judith Mackrell
(Collins, London, 1990)

The Oxford First Companion to Singing and Dancing.
by Kenneth and Valerie Mackleish
(Oxford University Press, London, 1982)

Becoming a Dancer
by Dianne Rayner
(Text Publishing Company, Melbourne, 1992)
The story of young dancers at the Australian Ballet School

Margot Fonteyn
by Rachel Stewart
(Hamish Hamilton, London,1988)

Dance
by Eleanor Van Zandt
(Wayland, Hove, 1988)

INDEX